Sparkleton
The Glitter Parade

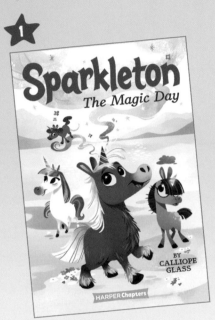
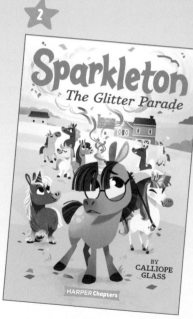

Sparkleton
The Glitter Parade

BY **CALLIOPE GLASS**

ILLUSTRATED BY
HOLLIE MENGERT

HARPER **Chapters**
An Imprint of HarperCollinsPublishers

To Whoozit,

the prettiest horse I ever loved.

Sparkleton #2: The Glitter Parade
Copyright © 2020 by HarperCollins Publishers
All rights reserved. Manufactured in China.
No part of this book may be used or reproduced in any manner whatsoever without
written permission except in the case of brief quotations embodied in critical articles
and reviews. For information address HarperCollins Children's Books, a division of
HarperCollins Publishers, 195 Broadway, New York, NY 10007.
www.harperchapters.com
Library of Congress Control Number: 2019950249
ISBN 978-0-06-294795-6 — ISBN 978-0-06-294794-9 (paperback)
The artist used Photoshop to create the digital illustrations for this book.
Typography by Andrea Vandergrift
20 21 22 23 24 SCP 10 9 8 7 6 5 4 3 2 1
❖
First Edition

TABLE OF CONTENTS

1: I Wonder What Kind of Magic I'll Get........1

2: Something Terrible Has Happened...........9

3: FireworksfireworksFIREWORKS (Part 1)....15

4: Maybe There Was a Mistake...............22

5: Better Than You, Sparkleton.............31

6: Throw Some Glitter on It................37

7: I Think I'm Feeling Positive............44

8: Where Did Gabe Go?....................48

9: *How* Dangerous?.......................55

10: I've Been Practicing!..................61

11: All I Have to Do Is Practice Really Hard?...66

12: Let Us Greet the Solstice.............72

13: FireworksfireworksFIREWORKS (Part 2)...81

1

I Wonder What Kind of Magic I'll Get

It was a sunny morning in Shimmer Lake. All the young unicorns were playing in the field during recess. Sparkleton was chasing Willow, who was hunting for pixies. Their friend Gabe was admiring a mushroom that had just sprouted at the base of a tree.

Suddenly, a whinny rang through the air—

"Did you hear?" Rosie asked. She galloped up to her friends. "Dale got his magic!"

"Whoa," said Zuzu. "What *kind* of magic?"

"Super-speed magic! He's off training with the other speed unicorns now."

"That means Dale will get to perform in the Solstice Parade!" Twinkle said. "Perfect timing! It's only three days away!"

Every year, the unicorns in Shimmer Lake celebrated the longest day of the year with a parade. Any unicorns who got their powers that year got to show them off in the grand finale at the very end of the parade. It was a really big honor.

I want super-speed magic!

Me too!

ZUZU

ROSIE

Super speed is kind of a weird fit for Dale. He's so clumsy!

I know! I hope he doesn't super-run into a tree.

Yeah. But he probably will.

WILLOW

SPARKLETON

GABE

3

"I'm glad *I* didn't get my magic," Gabe said. "I wouldn't want to be the grand finale in that parade. What if I messed up?" Then he heaved a big, gusty sigh. "Besides, I'm too busy trying to grow a giant mushroom. And it isn't going very well."

"*I* hope I get *my* powers soon," Britta said cheerfully. "I want to have flower-garden magic."

"*I'm* going to get wish-granting magic," Sparkleton said.

Now, he didn't know that for *sure*. You could never really know until you actually *got* your magic. But Sparkleton wanted wish-granting powers more than anything else in the whole world. He wanted wish-granting powers more than he wanted to watch his big sister, Nella, fall into a smelly bog. And that was a *lot*.

"Recess is over!" Gramma Una whinnied from across the field. "Gather round, younglings!"

"What kind of magic do you think *I'll* get?" Willow asked as they all trooped back across the field.

Zuzu tilted her head. "Maybe protection magic," she said. "Because you aren't afraid of anything."

That was true. Willow *wasn't* afraid of anything . . . not even things she should be afraid of, like heights. And goblins.

"I hope I get confetti magic," Zuzu said. She pointed her horn across the meadow at some of the older confetti unicorns. They were practicing their magic. Clouds of confetti, glitter, bubbles, and sparks flew up. "Just looking at them cheers me up!"

That was what confetti magic was for— making people happy.

Gabe shuddered. "Blech! That would be my worst nightmare."

Don't worry, Gabe. That will never happen. You're the **gloomiest** unicorn in Shimmer Lake!

7

"Welcome back," Gramma Una said. "Let's get to work!"

Class went by in a blur. Sparkleton couldn't stop thinking about how Dale had gotten his powers. Dale wasn't much older than Sparkleton. Did that mean Sparkleton was going to get *his* magic soon? His heart beat faster just thinking about it. He'd have *so much fun* granting everyone's wishes—and a few of his own!

You've read one chapter! Maybe YOU have super-speed MAGIC!

2

Something Terrible Has Happened

That evening, Sparkleton stared up at the stars instead of sleeping.

I want my magic, he thought. *I'm tired of waiting for it. Maybe if I can spot a falling star . . .*

Sparkleton had heard that falling stars could grant wishes. But how? What if he found a falling star and *ate* it? Would that give him wish-granting magic? *Could* you eat a fallen star? Maybe if you cooked it first . . .

Maybe with some nice clover on the side . . .

Sparkleton drifted off to sleep.

The next morning, a loud noise woke him up.

Crash! Crunch! Thud!

Someone was galloping through the woods . . . in his direction!

"*Help!*" Gabe neighed as he burst into the clearing where Sparkleton's family lived. Sparkleton had never seen him look so excited—or so alarmed!

"Whazza?" Gramma Una said, shaking her head and standing up from her grassy bed. "Gabe, are you okay?"

"Oh—" Gabe said, looking around. He seemed to come back to himself. His ears flopped down, his mouth drooped into a frown, and even his mane and tail seemed to sag. "Oh no," he said gloomily. "I woke you guys up."

"What happened?" Nella asked. She nudged Gabe with her nose. "Hey, you smell different," she said. "Like . . . like birthday cake sprinkles and the smoke from fireworks."

Gabe's ears went flat back on his head. "Sparkleton," he said, "I need to talk to you *in private*."

Sparkleton and Nella looked at each other. Sparkleton swished his tail in a unicorn shrug. It was his way of saying *I have no idea*.

Gabe led Sparkleton to his mushroom cave. By the time they got there, Gabe looked like he was about to cry.

"Something terrible has happened," Gabe said. Sparkleton's eyes went wide.

"I . . ." He gulped loudly and then went on:

I got my magic.

Sparkleton couldn't believe it.

"This is great news!" he said. He rushed over and bumped shoulders with Gabe in a unicorn hug.

Gabe didn't bump back. In fact, he almost fell over. Then he gave a miserable sniffle.

"Wait," Sparkleton said. "Why are you *sad*?"

"It's *confetti* magic," Gabe said.

"Oh *mud*!" Sparkleton said.

Gabe whinnied. "Now I have to make confetti in front of *everyone* at the Solstice Parade!"

3

Fireworksfireworks-FIREWORKS (Part 1)

Confetti magic was all about making people *happy*, which usually meant *being* happy. All the confetti unicorns Sparkleton had ever met were cheerful, silly, happy unicorns.

Gabe, on the other hand . . .

"I hate everything," Gabe said. "Here, watch this." He squeezed his eyes closed. A single, sad piece of confetti flew out of his horn.

Splat. It hit Sparkleton square on the nose.

Sparkleton winced. The confetti was cold and damp. It did not make Sparkleton feel happy. It made him feel like there was a slug on his nose.

"This *cannot* be my actual unicorn magic," Gabe said. "Sparkleton, I think there's been a terrible mistake."

"You're in luck! Terrible mistakes are my specialty!" a voice said from the mouth of the cave. Sparkleton turned to see Willow peering in the entrance.

"I heard your voices," she said. "What's going on? Gabe looks even gloomier than usual."

Sparkleton and Gabe explained the situation.

"I'm not sure if it's a *mistake*," Willow said. "I'm not sure magic can *make* mistakes." She tilted her head. "But you're right about one thing," she added.

"What?" Gabe said.

It IS terrible. Because the Solstice Parade is only TWO days away!

"Ugh," Gabe said. "I hate when other unicorns stare at me. Maybe I can run away and live with the goblins." His ears pricked. "They probably don't even know what parades *are*."

"I *love* this plan," Willow said. She pranced with excitement.

"Listen," Sparkleton told Gabe, "maybe it's not as bad as you think. Why don't you come out of the cave and give us another demonstration right now? I bet you'll get it this time."

Gabe sighed. "Okay," he said as he walked out of the cave. "But you aren't going to like it."

"Gabe," Willow said once they were in the field, "can you make me some fireworks?"

"I'll try," Gabe said. He pointed his horn at the air above Willow. He closed his eyes. "FireworksfireworksFIREWORKS," he muttered.

Golden, pink, and green fireworks shot out of Gabe's horn. But instead of lighting up the sky above Willow, they set fire to her mane!

"AGH!" Willow yelled. She dropped to the ground and rolled around to put out the flame.

"I'm sorry! I'm sorry!" Gabe yelled.

"Jump in the stream!" Sparkleton shouted. Willow's mane was still smoking. They galloped to a nearby stream, and Willow stuck her head and neck in.

Willow pulled her head out of the water. "I'm fine, Gabe," she repeated. "Don't worry."

"Oh, I'm worried," Gabe said. "I'm very, very worried. In two days, I'm going to be humiliated in front of every unicorn in Shimmer Lake!"

Sparkleton didn't say it out loud, but he thought Gabe was right to be worried.

This wasn't good.

WHAZZA! What do YOU think I'm going to do NEXT?

4

Maybe There Was
a Mistake

"**G**abe!" a cheerful voice called. The three friends turned. It was Twinkle. Ugh, Sparkleton *hated* Twinkle. She was so . . . *nice*.

"Congratulations!" she said as she galloped up to Gabe. She slid to a halt and bumped his shoulder in a unicorn hug. "I saw your fireworks just now! You got *confetti* magic? You're so lucky!"

Twinkle tried to bump his shoulder again,

but Gabe took a big side step away from her. She bumped the air instead and nearly fell over.

"Whoops!" Twinkle said. She staggered back upright. "You don't look so happy! Do you want some privacy? Should I go?"

Gabe nodded mutely.

"Okay, no problem!" Twinkle said. She flicked her tail at all three of them. "Bye, you guys! Have a glitterrific day! Feel better, Gabe!"

She trotted away.

"*She* should have gotten confetti magic," Gabe said. "Not me."

"Hmm," Willow said. "Maybe there really was a mistake. Maybe you got Twinkle's magic by accident."

"Or maybe it was a practical joke!" Sparkleton added.

"You *are* super gloomy, Gabe," Willow said. "Maybe someone is trying to cheer you up."

"Geez," Gabe said. "You think someone did this to me as a prank?"

"Not really," Willow said. "But you know my motto—"

"'There's no magic like goblin magic'?" Sparkleton asked.

"No, not that motto," Willow said.

"'If you're not in trouble, you're not living your best life'?" Gabe asked.

Willow had a lot of mottos.

"Not that one either," Willow said. "No, I mean, 'Leave no stone unturned.'"

"Oh," Sparkleton said. "The *boring* motto."

"Yep," Willow said. "Come on, Sparkleton, let's go turn over some stones."

"Count me out," Gabe said. "Ugh, I wish I'd just gotten mushroom magic." He turned and moped his way back into his cave. Sparkleton felt bad for his friend.

I WISH I could grant Gabe's wish.

"Yoo-hoo!" someone called loudly. Sparkleton and Willow turned around. A bunch of older confetti unicorns were galloping toward them.

"We heard Gabe got his magic!" one of them cried.

"We're going to have so much fun getting to know him!" yelled another.

"We can't wait to see what he's going to do at the Solstice Parade!" a third added.

"Wait until we teach him the confetti cheer!" said the first. "He'll love it!"

Confetti **is a party!**
Confetti is a fest!
It's hard **to** learn **at first,**
So **try** your **very best!**
YAAAAAAAYYYYYYY!

WHAM.

The confetti unicorns all went flying. Something moving incredibly fast had knocked them right over.

"I'm so sorry!"

It was Dale.

"Are you okay?!" Dale asked, trotting over to the pile of groaning confetti unicorns. He nosed one of them anxiously. "I can't believe I did that.  Well, actually, I can. I'm terrible at this."

"I'm sparkletastic!" the unicorn at the bottom of the pile said. "Don't worry!"

The confetti unicorns all picked themselves up and brushed themselves off.

"Tell Gabe we can't wait to meet him!" one of them said, swishing his tail cheerfully. Then they all trotted away.

"Gabe got *confetti* magic?" Dale asked. He shook his head. "Stars! And I thought *my* magic was a bad match."

"How are you doing?" Willow asked Dale. "Is being super speedy a lot of fun?"

"No, I keep crashing into things," Dale said. He hung his head sadly. "I'm really worried about the parade, you guys. I'm so bad at this!"

Then he tilted his head. "But you know who I feel *really* sorry for?" he added as he trotted away.

"Gabe."

5

Better Than You, Sparkleton

"We've got to get to the bottom of this," Willow said. Sparkleton nodded.

All Sparkleton wanted in the whole world was to have wish-granting magic. But maybe he could grant a wish *without* magic—Gabe's wish.

Gabe's confetti magic had to be a mistake . . . or a joke. Either way, Gabe didn't want it. And Sparkleton was determined to help his friend.

"I bet it was a practical joke," Willow said. "I bet someone just wanted to make Gabe smile."

"I don't think I've ever seen Gabe smile," Sparkleton said. "But I get why someone would want to try."

"Yeah," Willow agreed. "We might have a lot of suspects in this mystery."

But they were wrong.

"Gabe?" Nella said. "He's such a good unicorn. Better than you, Sparkleton. Gabe gave me a fancy mushroom one time. What have *you* ever given me? Anyway, I'd never prank him."

I love Gabe! He has such good manners, that boy. And pranks are VERY RUDE.

AUNT CORNELIA

"He always remembers my birthday," said Rosie. Then she snorted in an angry way and stamped a hoof. "You think someone's pranked him? I'll prank *them*! Nobody pranks Gabe on my watch!"

"Wow," Willow said to Sparkleton after they had interviewed everyone they could find.

"I guess it isn't a prank after all," Sparkleton said.

Willow flicked an ear thoughtfully. "Maybe Gabe was right," she said. "Maybe it *was* a mistake."

"Maybe *what* was a mistake?" someone asked. Sparkleton and Willow whirled around. It was Gramma Una.

"Gramma!" Sparkleton said. Gramma Una knew everything. She was the *perfect* unicorn to ask about Gabe's predicament. "Do you think Gabe got his confetti powers by mistake?"

"Yeah," Willow added, "can that happen?"

Gramma Una shook her head. "Nope," she said. "We get the powers we're going to get. It's like asking if you got a purple coat by mistake, Sparkleton."

Sparkleton and Willow looked at each other.

"So Gabe really has confetti powers?" Sparkleton said doubtfully.

"That just doesn't seem *right*," Willow said.

"Magic is mysterious!" Gramma Una said cheerfully. "Now quit talking to *me* and go talk to *Gabe*. He needs his two best friends right now."

6

Throw Some Glitter on It

"**R**ainbowrainbowRAINBOW*RAIN-BOW*!" Gabe shouted.

Sparkleton could hear Gabe from all the way across the field, even though Gabe was in his cave.

"He sounds frustrated," Willow said as they walked toward the cave.

"Well, I'd be annoyed, too, if I got confetti magic," Sparkleton said.

He shuddered at the thought. "Oh *glitter*, I hope I get wish-granting magic!"

"*RAINBOW-RAINBOWRAIN-BOW!*" Gabe shrieked from inside the cave.

"I've never heard Gabe scream before," Willow said. "Not even that time I dropped a spider into his ear."

"Me neither," Sparkleton said. "I'm glad we have a plan."

"Me too," Willow said.

Sparkleton and Willow reached the cave and peered inside. Gabe was pointing his horn at his mushroom garden. His eyes were squeezed shut. He was panting. But there was no rainbow to be seen. Instead, a cold, damp mist oozed from his horn. His mushrooms looked very happy. Gabe looked miserable.

"Gabe," Sparkleton said.

Gabe opened his eyes and sighed. "Oh, you're back," he said. "So who played this prank on me?"

"It's not a prank," Sparkleton told him.

"Gramma Una says you really have confetti powers," Willow said.

"So we came up with a plan," Sparkleton said. "We're going to help you figure out how to use them!"

"We think you should try to *be positive*," Willow said.

"Like the other confetti unicorns!" Sparkleton said. "They have a cheer and everything. You need to change your whole personality!"

Gabe winced. "But I don't *want* to change—" he started to say.

"Repeat after me," Sparkleton interrupted. "Confetti is a party!"

Gabe just stared at him.

"Gabe," Sparkleton said, "you have to do this! The Solstice Parade is in *two days*!"

"Fine," Gabe said. "Confetti is a party."

"Confetti is a fest!" Sparkleton said.

"Confetti is a fest," Gabe repeated slowly. He did not look festive.

Sparkleton tried to remember the next line of the confetti unicorns' cheer. He couldn't. So he started again.

"Confetti is a party!" he said.

Gabe lay down and put his head under an especially big mushroom. It dripped water on him. The water ran down his nose onto the ground.

"Confetti is a party," he said. His voice was muffled by the wet dirt.

Sparkleton looked at Willow. This wasn't working.

"Well," Willow said, "you know my motto."

"'There's no such thing as too many pixies'?" Sparkleton said.

"Good guess, but no," Willow said. "My other motto."

"'Throw some glitter on it'?" Gabe guessed.

Willow nodded. She liked that motto a lot.

"I've got a plan B," Willow said, "and it's all about glitter."

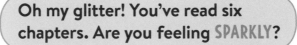

Oh my glitter! You've read six chapters. Are you feeling SPARKLY?

★ ★ ★ ★ ★ ★ 6 ☆ ☆ ☆ ☆ ☆ ☆ ☆

7

I Think I'm Feeling Positive

Willow led Gabe and Sparkleton to the base of a tall cliff on the shore of Shimmer Lake. There was a pool of pure glitter at the bottom of the cliff. It shimmered and glinted in the sun.

"I already hate this," Gabe said.

"All you have to do is climb the cliff and jump into the pool!" Willow said.

"That's a sparkletastic idea!" Sparkleton said.

"Being covered in glitter will make you feel more positive!"

Gabe stared at the pool of glitter. Then he looked up at the cliff. Then down at the pool again.

"That pool is awfully small," Gabe said nervously. Then he sighed. "But you aren't going to leave me alone until I try it, are you?" he asked.

Gabe climbed up
to the top of the cliff.
He stood there for
a moment. Then he
jumped.

SPLASH! He fell
straight into the pool.
Glitter sloshed all
over Sparkleton and
Willow. They burst
out laughing.

"Do you feel more
positive?" Sparkleton
asked.

"More confetti-y?"
Willow added.

Gabe swam to the
edge of the pool and
climbed out.

"I think so," he said. "Does feeling positive make your nose itch?"

"Uh," Sparkleton said. "I don't—"

"Does it make your eyes water?" Gabe added. "Because my nose is itching and my eyes are watering." He blinked rapidly.

"Guys. I think I'm feeling positive," Gabe said. His face twisted weirdly. Sparkleton held his breath. Was Gabe going to . . . *smile*?!

AH-CHOO! Gabe sneezed.

"Oh," Gabe said. He shook his head hard. Glitter flew out of his ears. "Wait, no," he said. "That was just a sneeze."

8

Where Did Gabe Go?

"Gabe!" someone yelled. "Look, guys, it's Gabe! Hey, Gabe!"

The confetti unicorns were trotting down the beach toward Sparkleton, Willow, and Gabe.

"Yoo-hoo!" one of them cried, swishing her tail in a friendly way. "Gabe! We want to give you some confetti advice!"

"Oh no," Gabe groaned. He plucked a big

reed from the edge of the glitter pond and jumped back in.

"Where did Gabe go?" the confetti unicorns asked, trotting up to the pool. "Wasn't he just with you?"

"We wanted to tell him something really important," one of them said. "Everyone thinks confetti magic must be so *easy* just because it looks so *fun*. But it actually takes a lot of—"

Sparkleton interrupted her. He pointed in the opposite direction with his nose. "I bet this 'Gabe' you're looking for is over there," he said.

"Thanks!" she said. "Come on, Team Confetti!"

And the confetti unicorns all trotted off.

When they were gone, Gabe dragged himself out of the glitter pond.

"*Ah-choo!*" he said, sneezing again.

He looked less positive than ever.

"This isn't working," Sparkleton said.

"Yeah," Willow said. "We need a new plan."

"I know!" Sparkleton said. "We should have a splash party in the glitter pool!"

He and Willow dove into the pool. They
pawed at the glitter with their front hooves. It
splashed everywhere!

"Is this supposed to help me?" Gabe asked,
annoyed.

"No," Sparkleton said. "Not at all! I just
thought it would be fun."

"And it is!" Willow said.

"Well," Gabe said. "As long as *you're* happy."

Happy. *Happy.*

Sparkleton leapt out of the pool.

"That's it!" he cried. "Remember when I had wish-granting powers for a day?"

"You mean the day I had a storm cloud attached to my head?" Gabe asked.

"Also known as the day I almost got to use goblin magic," Willow said dreamily.

"Remember why all the wishes I granted came out opposite?" Sparkleton asked. He didn't wait for them to answer. "Because I was thinking about myself more than the unicorns making the wishes. Maybe that's what Gabe is doing wrong! He has to think about making the *other* unicorns happy."

Gabe shrugged. "It's worth a try, I guess," he said.

He pointed his horn at Sparkleton and squeezed his eyes shut.

"Sparkleton," Gabe said. His voice was completely flat. "I really love you. You're one of my best friends. You're smart and you're funny. And when you step on the mushrooms in my garden, it's always by accident and never on purpose."

"That's true!" Sparkleton said.

"You're my friend, and I want you to be happy," Gabe said. He squeezed his eyes shut even tighter.

"RainbowrainbowRAINBOW!" he said.

A big, bright, colorful rainbow streamed out of his horn—

POW!

—and socked Sparkleton right in the face.

How Dangerous?

"**O**uch," Sparkleton said.

Gabe started to cry.

"That's quite a goose egg you've got there," Willow told Sparkleton. "We should probably go find you a unicorn with healing magic."

Sparkleton shook his head. The bruise on his face was throbbing, but he didn't want to leave Gabe. He was worried about his friend.

"I *hate* my magic," Gabe said through his tears. "It's supposed to cheer people up. But instead, it's setting my friends on fire and punching them in the face. And the parade is going to be a *complete disaster*! Dale and I are supposed to be the *grand finale*! Everybody's going to be watching. All of Shimmer Lake will see how terrible I am. I *wish to glitter* I'd gotten any other kind of magic!"

Gabe dissolved into sobs again.

Sparkleton and Willow stared at Gabe. Sparkleton had no idea what to do. He turned to Willow.

"I think . . ." Willow said, ". . . that it's time for some goblin magic."

"That sounds like a terrible idea," Sparkleton said.

"Yep!" Willow agreed. "It'll probably be a disaster . . ."

"But what if it isn't?" Sparkleton filled in. That was Willow's favorite motto.

"We're going to use a goblin spell to switch Gabe's powers from confetti magic to mushroom magic," Willow said. She started pacing up and down.

"I've been training for this moment my *whole life*. It's going to be awesome and also *very dangerous*."

"Glitterrific!" Sparkleton said. He pranced a bit, he was so excited. Willow was the best.

"Uh," Gabe interjected. He had stopped crying and now he just looked worried. "*How dangerous?*"

"It's *fine*," Willow said.

SIDE EFFECTS MAY INCLUDE: head on backward, no ears for one week, turn into a goblin, turn into TWO goblins, upside-down butterfly syndrome, electric teeth, and stomachache.

"Count me out," Gabe said. "I'll be in my mushroom garden with my head on the right way and non-electric teeth."

"Come *on,* Gabe," Willow said impatiently. "Don't be a *bunny rabbit.*"

Gabe stamped a hoof angrily. "I'm not a bunny rabbit. And I'm not a *positive* unicorn. And I'm not your test subject, either, Willow. I'm *me,* Gloomy Gabe, and *I'm sick of you trying to make me into something I'm not.*"

He started to turn away.

"Gabe, wait!" Sparkleton said.

"Just leave me alone!" Gabe yelled, and stomped away.

You must be FOCUSED. You've read NINE whole CHAPTERS!

10

I've Been Practicing!

"**W**ell, that didn't go great," Sparkleton said.

"Nope," Willow agreed.

"Hey, guys!" Dale said.

"Gah!" Sparkleton cried out. He jumped straight into the air, he was so startled. "Where did you come from?"

"I ran really fast!" Dale said. "And then I stopped—without crashing into anyone! Want to see me do it again?"

"Sure!" Willow said.

Dale took off. He ran so fast they could barely see him. Then he slid to a stop in front of a distant tree. He'd gone most of the way down the beach in under a second!

"Hi!" he yelled, rearing up. "I'm coming back now!"

"Oka—" Sparkleton started to call.

"Hi!" Dale said, sliding to a stop in front of Sparkleton.

"Gah!" Sparkleton blurted again. "Stars, Dale!"

"That was twinkletastic!" Willow exclaimed.

"I've been practicing," Dale said. "It turns out that even if you *have* a power, you might not be good at using it right away. That's why you have to practice! I think if I keep practicing really hard, I'll be able to run straight up the cliff wall by the time the parade happens!"

"This cliff wall?" Sparkleton asked. He nodded at the cliff over the glitter pool.

"Yep!" Dale said. "That's going to be my grand finale for the parade. Want to see me try right now?"

"Sure!" Sparkleton and Willow said together.

Dale backed up a few steps from the cliff face. Then he ran at it—and ran straight up it! For a moment it looked like he'd get all the way up to the top. But then he lost speed . . . and fell backward into the glitter pool.

SPLOOSH!

"See?" Dale said, popping up out of the glitter pool. "I almost made it! And if I keep practicing, I'll make it during the parade for sure!" He grinned. "I just have to *practice*!"

Sparkleton and Willow looked at each other.

"*Practice*," Sparkleton said. "That's it!"

"We have to find Gabe," Willow agreed.

"Bye, Dale! Practice hard!" Sparkleton said as he and Willow took off at a gallop toward Gabe's mushroom cave.

11

All I Have to Do Is Practice Really Hard?

Sparkleton and Willow found Gabe in the very back of his cave. He was lying in the dirt and talking to a snail.

"You're so lucky, Booger," Gabe told the snail. "Nobody's making *you* be in a parade."

The snail patted Gabe's nose with its feelers.

"Thanks," replied Gabe.

"Gabe!" Sparkleton called. The snail turned and slimed away.

"What?" Gabe answered. He didn't get up. He didn't even lift his head.

"Listen," Sparkleton said, "we got it all wrong. Getting the hang of your confetti magic is simpler than any of us realized."

"You just need to *practice*!" Willow cried. "That's why those other confetti unicorns keep coming around. They want to help you train!"

"I finally remembered the last two lines of the confetti cheer!" Sparkleton said.

Confetti is a party!
Confetti is a fest!
It's hard to learn at first,
So try your very best!

"They were trying to tell you it wasn't going to be easy right away," Willow said.

"You're terrible at confetti magic because it's *really hard*!" Sparkleton exclaimed.

Gabe lifted his head. "Wait a second," he said. "This isn't a prank and it isn't a mistake? And I don't have to learn to be more positive? Or jump in any more pools of glitter?"

"Right!" Sparkleton said.

"All I have to do is practice really hard?" Gabe asked.

"Yes!" Willow said.

"Okay," he said. "I'll do it."

"I'll go get the confetti crew," Sparkleton said. "Maybe they can help." He started for the entrance of the cave.

"No, wait!" Gabe stood up. Sparkleton stopped and turned around.

"I don't really know them," Gabe said. "And they're really . . ."

"Chirpy?" Sparkleton said.

"Chipper?" Willow asked.

"Cheery," Gabe said. "They're just . . . kind of overwhelming. The whole thing is overwhelming. I'm going to have to be in a *parade*. I hate parades!" He cleared his throat shyly. "I wish . . . Would you guys be willing to help me?"

"That is a wish I *can* grant!" Sparkleton said. "Even without wish-granting magic!" He bumped Gabe's shoulder. "Of course I'll help."

"Me too!" Willow said. "It's okay if I use goblin magic to help, right?"

"No," Gabe said.

Willow shrugged. "It was worth a try," she said. "Okay, I'm in!"

"You'll help me practice rainbows?" Gabe asked them.

"Yes!" Sparkleton and Willow said.

"You'll help me practice bubbles?"

"Uh-huh!" they answered.

"You'll help me practice fireworks?"

"No way!" Willow said. Then she laughed and poked Gabe with her horn. "Okay, fine," she added. "As long as we're standing in the lake."

12

Let Us Greet the Solstice

"**H**ow do you feel?" Sparkleton asked Gabe.

It was two days later, and they were walking down to the beach. The parade was starting soon, and Sparkleton was excited. Today was his favorite day of the year! He hoped Gabe would be able to enjoy it, too.

"I feel nervous," Gabe said. "But I guess it could be worse. All that practice really helped."

"You're doing the fireworks, right?" Willow asked.

"Yeah," Gabe said. "I've been practicing them for the last two days! Plus, I have an idea for something really special."

"What?" Sparkleton asked.

"It's a surprise," Gabe said. "It's something no other confetti unicorn has ever done."

The three friends headed down to the beach of Shimmer Lake. As they walked, more and more unicorns joined them. Soon, Sparkleton, Gabe, and Willow were in a huge crowd of unicorns. And before they knew it, the crowd had become a parade.

Musical unicorns sang and stomped their hooves in rhythm. Flying unicorns soared overhead. Wish-granting unicorns granted joyful wishes left and right. And the confetti unicorns led the parade. They sent confetti shooting into the air, and it rained down gently on all the unicorns that followed. A sparkly piece landed on Gabe's nose, and he sneezed.

Finally, at sundown, the parade reached its end. All the unicorns in Shimmer Lake gathered at the edge of the water. A hush fell over the crowd. Gramma Una climbed up onto a big rock.

"Welcome," she said. "Let us greet the solstice."

In one motion, all the unicorns reared up on their hind legs. And at that moment, the sun dipped below the horizon.

Sparkleton stayed up on his rear legs as long as he could. He pawed the air with his front hooves. It was hard to keep his balance, but he liked trying. This was his favorite part of the Solstice Parade.

Next to him, Gabe dropped back down onto all fours, and then Willow did as well. Soon all the unicorns in the crowd were standing and waiting for the grand finale.

"We have two guests of honor tonight," Gramma Una told everyone. "Two young unicorns have gotten their magic since our last Solstice Parade. Dale, Gabe, please join me."

Gabe and Dale both climbed up onto the rock with Gramma Una.

"Dale has speed magic," Gramma Una said. All the speedsters in the crowd stomped their hooves. "And Gabe has confetti magic." All the confetti magic unicorns sent up bubbles, confetti, glitter, and sparkles in celebration of Gabe. He blinked shyly.

"And now," Gramma Una said, "these two young unicorns will demonstrate their magic for us."

Dale took a deep breath. Then he began to run. He started at a normal speed. But by the time he reached the cliff, he was just a blur. And then, all of a sudden—

"Ta-da!" Dale yelled from the top of the cliff.

The crowd went bananas.

When the happy whinnies died down, Gramma Una turned to Gabe.

Gabe cleared his throat nervously and pawed at the sand a little bit. All the unicorns in Shimmer Lake waited in silence to see what he would do. Finally, after a long pause, he lifted his head.

"I have two demonstrations," Gabe announced in a soft voice. "One of them is fireworks."

Everyone cheered. Unicorns love fireworks.

"The other," Gabe said, "is something that means a lot to me." He squared his shoulders. "You might all hate it, but I still think it's neat."

Sparkleton and Willow looked at each other. Was this Gabe's big surprise?

What could it be?!

"This might end in disaster," Willow said under her breath. She crossed her ears—the unicorn version of crossing your fingers for good luck.

Sparkleton grinned. "But what if it doesn't?" he answered. And Willow smiled back, reassured.

But when she wasn't looking, Sparkleton crossed his ears, too.

Only one more chapter to go!
Are you ready for the GRAND FINALE?

12

13

Fireworksfireworks-FIREWORKS (Part 2)

Gabe climbed down from the big rock and went around behind it. He reappeared, tugging a big wagon behind him. And in the wagon was a giant flowerpot.

And in the flowerpot was the biggest mushroom Shimmer Lake had ever seen. It was the size of a full-grown unicorn. It was purple with pink spots, and it smelled like seaweed.

There was a confused silence from the unicorns of Shimmer Lake.

"This is my record-setting *Agaricus corneolus*," Gabe said. "Confetti magic is all about making others happy. Well, I use mine to make this mushroom very happy. See?"

Gabe squeezed his eyes shut.

"Coldmistcoldmistcoldmist," he muttered.

A clammy fog came out of his horn. The mushroom gleamed happily. Sparkleton could swear he *saw* it growing.

Gabe turned to the crowd of unicorns.

coldmistcoldmistcoldmist

"I know this mushroom stuff is only exciting to me," he said. "So now I'll give you some—"

"Hooray for Gabe's mushroom!" Sparkleton yelled.

"Huh?" Gabe said, surprised.

"Three cheers for the *Agaricus corneolus*!" Willow cried.

"Hip! Hip!" Sparkleton yelled.

"Hooray!" all the unicorns of Shimmer Lake answered. It was a deafening roar.

As Sparkleton watched, Gabe did something Sparkleton had never seen him do before.

He smiled.

"Okay," Gabe said. "Okay, okay, okay. Time for fireworks." He pointed his horn up toward the sky and closed his eyes.

"FireworksfireworksFIREWORKS!" he said.

Several flashes of light flew into the inky night sky. They exploded in a shower of sparks.

Sparkleton blinked.

"I can't see what shape the fireworks are," he said to Willow. "Can you?"

"No," she said. "They're too bright!"

But then their eyes got used to the light, and they saw—

"Ha!" Willow exclaimed, smiling in delight. "Gabe's fireworks are *frowny faces*!"

Sparkleton and Willow burst into laughter.

The rest of the crowed stomped for joy.

"Gabe didn't have to change his personality to match his confetti magic!" Sparkleton pointed out. "He changed his confetti magic to match his personality!"

The confetti magic unicorns all grouped around Gabe. They began chanting . . . but this time it was a new version of their chant.

Gabe brought a mushroom to the party!
And frowny fireworks to the fest!
It's the funnest solstice ever,
Because Gabe's the very best!
YAAAAAAAYYYYYY!

And Gabe smiled . . .
Again!

CONGRATULATIONS!

You've read **13** chapters,

87 pages,

and **6,230** words!

Feeling **GLIMMERTASTIC**?

Which Sparkleton book will you read **NEXT**?

If you read books one *and* two, **YOU'VE READ** 25 chapters, 174 pages . . .

. . . and 11,902 words! **KEEP AT IT**!

UNICORN GAMES

THINK!

If you could have any unicorn power, what would it be and why? Draw a picture of yourself using your magic to help someone else. Or write a song about it!

FEEL!

Think of a time when you felt like you could not be yourself. How did that make you feel? Write about it in your journal or share your story with a friend.

ACT!

Need a cheer? Never fear! Make up a cheer with your friends to inspire each other to always do your very best. Does your cheer have dance moves to go along with it?

CALLIOPE GLASS is a writer and editor. She lives in New York City with two small humans and one big human, and a hardworking family of house spiders who are all named Gwen. There are no unicorns in her apartment, but they are always welcome.

HOLLIE MENGERT is an illustrator and animator living in Seattle. She loves drawing animals, making people smile with her work, and spending time with her amazingly supportive family and friends.